This Storybook Belongs To

Princess **Miranda**

Getting to Know You

ADVANCE PUBLISHERS

"Maybe the Beast has a heart, after all," thought Belle. That very day, he had rescued her from a pack of wolves in the forest. Even though the Beast was angry with Belle for having left the castle against his orders, he had chosen to risk his own life to save hers.

"Maybe I could try a little harder to be his friend," she told herself. "He certainly looks harmless now. Poor dear."

Mrs. Potts, Lumiere, and Cogsworth were hopeful. If the Beast and Belle fell in love, the spell that had turned the castle's inhabitants into household objects would be broken—and they would be human again!

That night, Mrs. Potts went to where the Beast sat brooding in his room. "Master, it's such a chilly night," she began. "How about a nice, hot drink in front of the fireplace? I'm sure Belle would love some company."

"As long as the company isn't me," said the Beast with a sigh.

"Nonsense, Master," replied Mrs. Potts. Reluctantly, the Beast followed.

The Beast stomped into the sitting room and settled himself in a chair.
Belle looked up. "Good evening," she said.
The Beast did his best to smile politely.

Belle went back to her reading until she was startled by a loud SLURP. She glanced at the Beast.

The Beast quickly stopped drinking and slumped in his chair.

Mrs. Potts tried to change the subject. "Why don't you read to us, dearie?"

"Once upon a time there was an old woodcutter—" Belle began.
"That sounds so boring!" interrupted the Beast.
Mrs. Potts asked gently, "Is there another story, Belle?"
Belle flipped through the pages until she found a tale filled with fire-breathing dragons and brave knights. The Beast sat on the edge of his seat, listening to every word, and when he started to drink his tea again, he took care to sip instead of slurp.

The next day, Lumiere and Cogsworth decided to play matchmakers, too.

"What a beautiful day for a walk!" Cogsworth said after breakfast.

"What's the point of taking a walk?" challenged the Beast. "Walking is useful only when you have somewhere to go!"

But before Belle and the Beast knew it, they were bundled into their winter cloaks and herded outdoors.

"There's nothing more romantic than a walk in the snow!" Lumiere sighed dreamily.

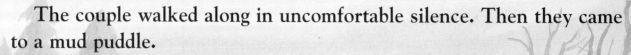

The couple walked along in uncomfortable silence. Then they came to a mud puddle.

"A gentleman would carry me over," Belle thought. Clearly, the Beast wouldn't.

"Oh, well, here I go!" she thought as she waded through the mud.

The wind picked up, and all at once it
started to snow. "It looks as if a bad
storm is coming," the Beast warned.
"We'd better get back while we can
still see where we're going."

Quite unexpectedly, the Beast took
her hand. "Follow me!" he commanded,
leading her through the blizzard.

Lumiere and Cogsworth were watch-
ing out the window as the two
approached, Belle's hand firmly grasping
the Beast's paw.

"How romantic!" exclaimed Lumiere.

"It looks as if you and the Master are getting to know each other better,"
said Mrs. Potts casually as the Wardrobe helped Belle out of her muddy clothes.
Belle hesitated. "I suppose," she answered. "There is so much about him
that's gruff and rude...yet, he's full of surprises."

In the meantime, in another part of the castle, the Beast told Cogsworth, "Belle can be rather boring and proper. But, then again, she walked through the mud without complaining. And she didn't act scared at all when we got caught in the storm. She's...kind of surprising."

That afternoon, Mrs. Potts prepared a lovely picnic lunch and served it in the greenhouse of the castle.

"Remember, Master," Lumiere coached the Beast beforehand, "young ladies appreciate politeness."

"Try to be understanding, Belle," begged Mrs. Potts in another room. "The Master's manners aren't always what they should be—but he's trying!"

Finally, at the table, Belle smiled, and the Beast grinned unconvincingly. Both were tired of trying to be on their best behavior.

The Beast picked up a chicken leg and began to devour it.

But after Belle picked up her napkin and placed it in her lap, the Beast hurriedly grabbed his own napkin and did the same.

"Isn't this lunch delicious?" asked Belle.

"Mmpffgrl," answered the Beast, his mouth stuffed with food.

Just then he noticed his napkin on the floor. He ducked down to retrieve it—and accidentally tipped the table over as he tried to sit back up.

A roll went shooting off the Beast's plate and over to Belle.

"Uh-oh," thought the Beast. Even he knew that throwing food was not polite. He was about to apologize when he saw a playful smile on Belle's face. To his surprise, she pitched the roll back over the table at him!

When Mrs. Potts, Lumiere, and Cogsworth came to check on the pair, they couldn't believe their eyes. The room was a mess, and, even more peculiar, Belle and the Beast were laughing!

Mrs. Potts smiled knowingly. "I think they discovered what we forgot: The real way to make friends is to relax and be yourself!"

Belle and the Beast shared a perfectly wonderful dinner that evening.

Afterward, Belle patiently taught the Beast how to dance. He listened carefully to everything she told him, and soon the two were gliding across the dance floor...in step with each other at last.